Praise for *Beyond the Veil*

"This short story was beautifully written. It is fantasy and the world is so well described that I felt I could see it. I will definitely be reading (more) books and stories by this author to see more of this world!"

~ *Anne, Goodreads*

"Christine Schulze pens a short story that I longed for it to go on..."

~ *Linda, Goodreads*

"The characters have unique voices that make the story very realistic. What I liked most about this story was the original ideas. This consisted of the magical ideas in the world-building and the magical aspects in the love story. They were unique ideas and very beautiful."

~ *Steven Guscott, Goodreads*

"'Beyond The Veil' is a magical story about love that can be found in unexpected places."

~ *Cathleen, Goodreads*

"I really enjoyed reading Beyond the Veil
I only wished that it was longer...
Cant wait to read more. "

~ *Terri Jackson, Goodreads*

BEYOND THE VEIL, 2ⁿᵈ Edition

Christine E. Schulze
Copyright © 2015
Cover Art by Christine E. Schulze © 2011
Back Cover Art by Tiffany Tutti © 2015
Edited by Christine E. Schulze

Author's Note: Of Macroworlds and Microworlds

Many of my stories take place in many different worlds—including our own. Places such as Loz, Hyloria, the Lynn Lectim Academy, and the Surpriser Kingdoms all root their history and settings in our world of Earth. But there are other worlds, such as Sulaimon from *Bloodmaiden* and Bienvinette from *Golden Healer, Dark Enchantress*.

What are these worlds? Do they have a set number, or are they limitless?

It is said that, at the beginning of time, Amiel, great Lord and Creator of all worlds (He is sometimes given other names in other worlds), created eight Macroworlds. These worlds are all accessible to each other, all interconnected. They are known as Earth, Novalight, Allyslies, Sulaimon, Bienvinette, Emreal, Fairie, and Etymology (the last of which is known also as "the first world" and better known simply as "the Elemental World"). Each world has its own races, history, and, in some cases, magical dynamic. For example, the world of Fairie is a phoenix world. It dies in ash and flame every five hundred years, only to be resurrected anew; thus its cycle will continue until the end of time.

Travel between Macroworlds is possible via certain magical portals, doors, spells, and other types of magic. Travel occurs often between the magical peoples of some worlds and rarely between others, though the eight Macroworlds all have some knowledge of one another. Non-magical humans have also been known to travel between worlds on occasion, either accidentally or because of great need.

The Microworlds are often much smaller. A Microworld can only be reached through the Macroworld in which it is housed. In *Lily in the Snow*, readers discover the Microworld of the dragon fairies. This world is a part of the Macroworld Etymology and can only be reached through Etymology. One could not find the Microworld of the dragon fairies from Novalight or Emreal or one of the other eight Macroworlds.

Well, there it is. A bit of lore on the many worlds, among which ours plays only a small part. Perhaps you may find yourself stumbling into one of these other realms someday. In the meantime, please continue to enjoy their stories which, as you will see in the end, are just as much a part of your own story.

Beyond the Veil

Beyond the Veil

Christine E. Schulze

Beyond the Veil

My Dearest Gailea,

This booklet, forged from journal entries and letters, is the account of my life over the past year and a half. I am Gillian, the Lady of Adelar, whose life before the time I wrote this seemed so very small, insignificant, and hopeless. I write this account because the time may come when I may have to sacrifice my life—and thus ours—for the fight for freedom your father and I have strived to lead the past couple of years. I pray that as you read it, my sweet daughter, you shall find hope and understanding. Your father and I would have never given you up willingly. You are our heart, and we love you with all of ours.

$\mathcal{D}$iary $\mathcal{E}$ntry 1

So many times. So many times I'd stood before the door to the forbidden room, debating whether or not I should go in. And so many times, I had given in. But today was different. Today was the day I felt that if I went through that door, I might never want to come out ever again.

I had fought with my father, King Weston of Adelar, for the last time—I was not going to marry Donyon. Donyon may have been Father's chief council man and like the son Father had never had, but he was not for me. I could not marry such a bitter, unfeeling soul. And yet, where could I go, how could I resist the bidding of a man who was not only my father, but the king as well? King over both my kingdom, the only home I had ever known, and my very life.

There was only the door and the room. They had been my only means of escape from the suffocating walls of the castle for many years, and they seemed my only, if temporary, escape now. I slipped inside and noiselessly shut the door behind me.

The cavernous room's ceiling was supported by elegantly carved pillars. As ever, I admired their craftsmanship in passing. I passed statues, maps on the walls, and soon came to my favorite section: the library of forbidden books. I glided past shelf upon shelf of books speaking of the worlds beyond the borders of Adelar, places like Loz, Hyloria, and other of Zephyr's Islands. I'd often wondered why the books—and the worlds they spoke of—should be so forbidden. Was it such an unforgivable crime to desire to step beyond my insular, narrow-minded kingdom, to be free to make my own choices for once? What was the worst that could happen to me? That the engagement might be broken off? Very well, so I would be alone. I'd always believed I would be anyway, for to marry Donyon would make me feel more alone than I ever was before.

Finally, emerging beyond the bookshelves, I stopped and looked.

There it was: my way to freedom.

In the middle of the room stood a golden archway, on which was hung a white silky curtain stretching to the floor. I knew what it was, for I'd read about them in one of the books of the Forbidden Room. It was one of the Veils the fairies and elves of old had scattered across the eight Spectrum Isles, to be used when the need arose to escape enemies or swiftly deliver important messages. It was unknown how many such Veils had survived after the mad king burned them along with many of the sorcerers who had created them. I sometimes wondered if mine was the last standing.

The Veil beckoned me forward. Though there were no windows in the room, it swayed gently, as if a breeze blew from within. I reached out and clutched its silky softness in one hand. Then I slipped inside, into the dark.

Though surrounded by complete blackness, I did not feel afraid. Rather, I felt excited, drawn forward by the thrilling unknown and not entirely of my own will; the Veil seemed to have a will of its own, for I somehow knew that I could not turn back now that I had started. But even this lack of control did not scare me. I was glad for the Veil's guidance and trusted it, as long as it took me away from the home that had become such a prison.

I crept slowly, carefully forward, hand outstretched. My fingertips brushed against something soft. Hand trembling, I drew aside a second Veil and stepped outside.

Hazy sunlight washed over me. The thick branches overhead filtered the sunlight, creating thin but pleasantly warm, glowing pillars. I barely had time to take anything else in because the next moment, someone shouted, "Watch out!"

I plunged to the ground, throwing my arms over my head as something massive swooped from the sky. A great rush of wind chilled me as the huge something soared scarcely a yard above my body. And then, the next moment, everything fell silent.

Slowly, I looked up and stared in amazement. Standing only a few feet away was a giant eagle. His feathers shone a deep golden-brown, except for his head, which was snowy white. Most mesmerizing of all was the almost blinding glint of his eyes. One glowed bright blue, the other deep red; both sparkled with hundreds of tiny facets, as though his eyes were actually embedded with a sapphire and ruby. They reflected a sense of power, and the eagle himself stood with his strong shoulders thrown back, head lifted high.

As I rose to my feet, I noticed a young man on the eagle's back, still hunched down and clutching onto the eagle's feathers for dear life. Whether his grip was due to the ride itself, the landing, or both, I could not tell, but he seemed either too frightened or else too shocked to realize they had stopped. So I called quietly, "Are you all right?"

He looked up. His brows rose as his glance caught me. "Oh, yes, thank you. Just a moment."

He slid off the eagle's back and proceeded to brush off his breeches; they didn't look dirty, but he kept moving his hands in swift, erratic patterns until he seemed quite sure of this himself. He looked up then, strawberry blonde curls glistening, vivid blue-green eyes studying me closely; these features made me wonder if he might be a Scintillate, from Rosa specifically. He took deep breaths as if trying to calm still-trembling nerves. His hands twitched, as if in a desire to keep brushing the flawless pants. Then, watching me, he smiled shakily and said, "I am sorry if I frightened you."

"Umm…it's all right," I assured, though I felt a bit uncomfortable being stared at with such interest. "Are you sure you're all right?"

"Yes, quite—what are you?" he blurted.

"I—I'm an Adelaran. And," I added with a playful smile, "my name is Gillian, if you'd like to know."

"Forgive me," he mumbled, his face turning a shade of red that nearly matched that of his wild curls. "That's what I had meant. I'm not usually such an incoherent fool, only the ride befogged me. Gillian is a lovely name. Mine is Callum. But the Adelarans—forgive me," he repeated, "I'm terribly curious about races outside my own—aren't they the people who are each born with a different magical power?"

I nodded. "Yes. Unlike most peoples, who are known for a certain signature magic, an Adelaran may be born with any power."

"May I ask what your power is?"

"Certainly." His nervousness put my own at ease, and I was suddenly glad to speak to someone who found me interesting for once, or for that matter, someone who spoke to me at all rather than ordering me around. "My power has to do with my music. I can hypnotize people with my music, make them do things."

His eyes widened. "Truly? Can you show me?"

I was surprised to be so quickly trusted by a stranger. "Are you certain?"

"Why, yes. You'll do me no harm, I take it." He smiled; mischief lit his eyes as he gestured toward the massive eagle behind him. "And I daresay the Eagle of Spectrum will defend me if you do."

I smiled back. "I promise no harm will befall you."

Then, after some quick thought, I began to whistle. Slowly, Callum stepped forward. His eyes glazed over, and he looked truly mesmerized. My whistling trailed as he stopped right before me, so close that I only now realized how tall he really was. As I studied his eyes, I saw too that they shone with an even more vivid interest and watchfulness.

"You know," he said quietly, "you didn't have to do that."

"Do what?" I said, my voice suddenly hushed to match his.

"Use your powers for that purpose; your charm and talent are enough to have beckoned me."

For a few moments, we stood in silence, simply gazing into each other's eyes. My heart raced. I had never seen such a look in anyone's eyes, nor had I ever felt this way about anyone. I wasn't sure what it meant, and it both frightened and exhilarated me all at once. I knew it couldn't be love—I'd never believed in love at first sight. But infatuation, perhaps, and maybe even friendship. Perhaps it was simply because he seemed to share my curiosity and boldness, or perhaps it was something more that I couldn't yet define.

Finally, I glanced away to take in my surroundings. We stood in a glen, in the midst of a dense forest. The trees were tall and the branches broad, providing a canopy that allowed only thin streams of sunlight to enter, yet the clearing was very bright. The trees, as well as the surrounding bushes, were covered in white blossoms, the petals of which had not yet opened.

"What is this place?" I breathed.

"I don't know. I've never been here before. Have you?"

"No."

Again, silence passed between us. There was a moment when I glanced up only to look quickly away from his deep, powerful eyes; they held an enchanting quality all their own, no magic needed.

At last he spoke. "So, how did you come to be here?"

I told him all about the Veil and the Forbidden Room—omitting anything about my father, Donyon, or any of my troubles. I ended by explaining my need to be free of my people's narrow-minded ways.

"Yes." Callum nodded. "I can understand that. My people are every bit as prejudiced as yours."

My eyes widened. "But by your looks you seem to be a Scintillate, are you not? I had not heard that they could be so bigoted. I've read in books about Loz that the Scintillates are explorers, filled with curiosity about the world around them—"

"I am a Scintillate—partly—but not from Loz. I am from Rosa, and I fear my land has been instilled by prejudice for many long years. Was I not a son of a renowned knight, I would have surely been exiled by now. Not that exile would be such an awful fate..."

"Then you understand," I said, in awe of the fact anyone could feel as I did. "You understand my loneliness, my longing for—"

"For freedom," he said quietly.

Our eyes met again. This time, his watchfulness did not make me so uncomfortable; rather, I watched him just as closely. We held this gaze for a long time, wondering and searching for our new but already strong understanding. I could still hardly believe that, so quickly, I'd formed such a bond with a stranger—someone who shared my own dreams for freedom.

"Why can't you just use your powers?" he asked quietly. "To escape?"

I glanced away. Moments ago, we'd been sharing our hearts, we'd been one in our quest for freedom. I wasn't so willing to let that moment end, so I chose a quick, curt reply, "Those who cage me have powers of their own, or else have the power to block mine." Father had never been swayed by my song, and Donyon was too keen at finding hidden truths.

I looked up. Callum accepted my answer with a quiet nod and said no more on the subject.

After a time, we sat beneath one of the trees and talked. For what seemed like hours, we spoke of music, of books—we found that we both liked to write stories and compose songs, and Callum said we should trade them some time.

"That is," he added with a hopeful glance, "if you'd like to meet again."

"Oh, yes," I said, blushing at my own eagerness. But he only smiled, and I smiled back. I felt, for the first time in ages, that I could be myself around someone. I could talk freely, smile, even laugh without anyone taking offense. And with his friendly, playful talk, he kept me laughing.

In the midst of our conversation, the eagle nuzzled its head between us. I jumped in surprise, but then he caressed my face with his soft feathers, as if apologizing.

"He seems to like you," Callum said.

"Where did he come from?" I asked.

"From Rosa, of course, just like me. Where else would he have come from, silly?"

15

Callum smiled playfully, and I lifted my chin in mock hauteur. "You speak too boldly with the daughter of a king!"

"I beg your pardon, milady." He seemed genuinely abashed. "I admit I feel very comfortable in your presence, and perhaps I have let myself be too free with my words. I promise I'll be more courteous—"

"No! Please don't!" I automatically reached out to grasp his hand, my fingers almost shocked by the touch of his warm skin before shyly letting go. "I was but teasing you. I—I like the way you talk to me."

His smile returned, and it was warmer; not as playful, but far more meaningful. "I am glad," he said softly.

The moment threatened to turn into another heavy silence and I hastened to break the spell lest things go too far between us. "Then tell me more about the eagle," I blurted. "And how you came here, to this place."

"Very well," Callum said, though his eyes twinkled as if he knew why I'd spoken so quickly. "Zephyr eagles are very rare, but a couple of them are born every now and then in Rosa, and the strongest is an appointed guardian of our kingdom. Originally, they were meant just to protect us, but now, they are only one of very few ways to breach the four barriers that now surround Rosa—two massive walls of water and two of fire. Breaching the barriers without the eagles involves advanced, complex magic, difficult for even the sharpest mind to understand. So I stole into the Treasury, obtained the Eagle's Song. The song is a summons, a spell of sorts that is required by any who wish to command him, else he'll follow no one's will but his own. Anyway, the song doesn't require a musical magician; anyone of Rosan blood can play and use it. So I played the song, the Eagle brought me here, and here I am."

16

"The Eagle's Song..." I reflected aloud, completely engrossed in his tale.

"Yes, shall I hum it for you?"

I nodded.

He hummed it a few times—he had a rich, deep voice—and I deposited it carefully to my memory.

"Do you like it?" he asked.

"Very much so."

"Good. Though I admit it does sound a good deal better when played on my lute."

My eyes lit up. "A lute? That's one of my favorite instruments. Perhaps you could bring it to play next time."

Callum's smile turned wry, and he glanced away. My heart fell a little despite myself. Stranger though he may be, I would already call him more of a friend and kindred spirit than anyone who lived at the castle with me.

When Callum looked at me again, the hard edge in his gaze had softened. "I would truly like to see you again. I'm just not certain how possible that might be. You see, I'm actually helping to head a rebellion in Rosa, to end the prejudices I spoke of. Tensions are rising and there have been some frightening acts committed in the name of demanding unity throughout the land. People are put to death for treason for the smallest slights—or, in many cases, on the mere whims of the king—just because they are not of pure Scintillate blood.

"I have been using the eagle to travel and rally followers, to make plans for our rebellion. However, doing so is risky; each time I escape, I risk capture and imprisonment. I know that the king's spies are *suspicious of a rebellion, though whether or not they are suspicious of me remains to be seen..."*

He sighed and shook his head. "I suppose I just don't want to make any promises. But if I can, I will come to you again. Tomorrow I have journeys to make for the rebellion. I will try to meet you here at sunset. Our time and the time here seem one and the same."

I nodded slowly, full of thought. "Is there...is there anything I could do? To help with the rebellion?"

Callum's brows rose. He looked not so much surprised, but amused. "You and I are truly alike. You would seize opportunity to aid a stranger like myself, if for the cause of justice and freedom so long-ago abandoned by our people. But how do you know I'm not really some enemy spy?"

I gazed at him seriously. "Perhaps I am just in a circumstance where I do not have so many choices—or time to choose—when it comes to whom I trust. Perhaps I just have to trust my intuition and believe that whatever you are doing is the possible path of freedom I've sought."

Callum didn't say a word, nor did he need to. The expression on his face reflected my thoughts: time was running out fast for the both of us. Indecision truly was not an option.

Glancing at the darkening sky, I said, "I should get going before I'm found missing."

"Then I shall escort you back to the Veil."

As he helped me to my feet, I looked up and gasped.

"The Veil! It's gone."

He grinned. "No, it's not. See those two trees, so perfectly straight and   parallel to each other?"

I nodded.

"Through there lies your Veil; some of the Veils were made like that, so that one entrance was disguised. Don't worry, you'll get back."

I was more worried about not ever getting back here, but I kept this thought to myself.

"Until tomorrow, then, perhaps?" I asked hopefully.

"Yes," he said, "if Amiel grants it." He gently kissed my hand. "Goodnight, Lady Gillian."

"Goodnight."

He threw himself on the back of the eagle and disappeared into the night sky. The eagle's eyes shimmered and then vanished into the ocean of stars.

I watched the sky a few moments more and then walked between the trees, through the darkness, and out of the Veil into the Forbidden Room. I wandered half dazed back to my bedchamber, readied for bed, and snuggled beneath the covers. But before going to sleep, I prayed. First, I thanked Amiel for blessing me with the friend I had so desperately needed. Then, I prayed he had not really been just a dream after all.

Diary Entry 2

Good tidings are upon me. I have learned that the young man I met last night was not a dream. He is very real, though at first, I was given great reason to doubt.

I returned to the Veil and our clearing the next night as agreed between us. I was trapped beforehand by meetings with Father and Donyon; thus, I could not steal to our clearing until far past sunset.

That night, the crescent moon had just risen and I watched with breathless wonder as the tiny white buds covering the trees around me opened their petals atmoonlight's first touch, bedazzling the branches like glistening snow. I felt a little sad that Callum was not by my side to witness this miracle, but I was eager to show him once he came.

After waiting a couple of hours, I knew he would not come and went back. It was a risky move, because I do not know all the rounds that the guards take around the castle at such a late hour, and I was almost spotted on several occasions making my way to my room.

I returned each night afterward, again risking much. As the days passed, I began to worry that he might have come to some harm because of our secret meetings.

Finally, after a week, though he still did not come, a small gray bird waited in the tree we'd sat beneath that first night. A piece of parchment was rolled up and secured in its beak. It was a note from Callum. He apologized for being unable to come, but the king of Rosa grew increasingly suspicious of their rebellion and had tightened *security in Rosa. Sneaking out would have been too risky, not just to Callum, but especially to the other members of the rebellion. Their safety depended on his actions, and he wouldn't place them in that kind of danger.*

He said, however, that I could write as often as I liked. He knows magic that allows our letters to safely reach each other.

Diary Entry 3

Over the past couple of months, Callum and I have written each other. I have told him now about Donyon and Father and my own needs for freedom. He responds with care and understanding; his encouragement speaks to my soul. In our letters, we hearten one another, telling little jokes or coming up with silly rhymes and songs, at other times simply describing our day's routine. We treat our correspondence like two friends simply talking to each other. Or, as time passes, like two friends hoping to court one another. I often feel like he is right beside me, and though I do ache for his physical presence, the feelings growing inside me toward him simply from our correspondence couldn't be more real.

However, I continue to take things slowly as I sort out my true feelings. True, Callum and I have many things in common, and a strong bond even through just our letters, but I don't want to say too hastily that what I feel may be love.

However, perhaps it is just fear that makes me deny the feelings which are otherwise so obviously true. My body is changing. This only happens to Adelarans, when we give our hearts to another of a different race—though the change will not be permanent unless we give ourselves physically to another. My hair begins to darken, turning auburn like his. I keep it in tight braids or swept into elegant buns adorned with beads, hoping Donyon does not take note; I know Father is too distracted to notice. My grey eyes also are flecked with hints of blue or green from time to time, depending on if I'm frightened or happy, and especially when I think of Callum. I cannot hide my eyes, nor can I stop the Adelaran birthmark on my arm from slowly fading away. Ultimately, if we make love, even much of my musical power will be transferred to him.

The signs are clear. I have given my heart to Callum. I am becoming a Scintillate like him. I am excited by the thought, but fear overshadows what would be elation. I will not be able to hide these signs much longer, and, should a physical union take place, there is no going back for an Adelaran, even if I wanted to. I do not know how Father or—Amiel forbid—Donyon will react. But, sooner or later, a rebellion of my own must and will take place within the very walls of this castle.

Diary Entry 4

After a few weeks of no correspondence from Callum, I began to fear the worst. I spent far more time in the Glen than I should have, risking much in hopes of seeing a letter fall from the sky, or him upon the Eagle once more.

Finally, after a week, the grey bird returned. It carried a note from Callum which said he'd been found out, caught, and captured one night when he'd tried to flee to see me again. He'd made no mention of me to the Scintillates, but his other plans had been found out. Many of his fellow rebellion leaders were already imprisoned or put to death. Only his father's favor kept Callum from execution; instead, he was banished to a lifetime of solitude inside one of the castle towers. He knew no magic that could free him of the tower, but he did have ways of communicating with the birds and other animals in the forests surrounding the castle. He'd sent word so that I could know he was safe.

I wrote him back, consoling the loss of his friends. I spoke nothing of my own situation, my own dire news, but time is not on my side either. Like a maiden hiding an undesired conception, it will soon be impossible for me to hide the physical signs of my affection for Callum.

Another grave piece of news confirms yet another fear of mine: Father and Donyon have been plotting behind my back again, and, as feared, the wedding draws inevitably closer. I must meet with

Donyon and Father today. I pray it goes better for me than the manner in which Callum's people have dealt with him.

Diary Entry 5

I gathered with Donyon and Father in his chambers. They discussed various matters, most of which I found uninteresting, until the talk turned to—

"The wedding," Father said, flashing his well-practiced smile. "We must make plans for the wedding."

Donyon's gaze looked deeply pensive, brooding but otherwise unreadable as usual.

I spoke slowly, scarcely controlling my voice from shaking, "The wedding? That's not for another year. Why plan it now?"

"It's never too soon to make plans, is it?"

"Your highness, we should tell her," Donyon said quietly. "She has a right, after all."

"Very well then," my father sighed. "Go on."

"Your highness," Donyon said as he turned his somber gaze upon me. "We've moved the wedding forward."

For a while, I could only stare. As if I wasn't stifled enough. The wedding being farther away had given me hope of holding on to what little freedom I yet possessed.

"I thought we were going to delay the wedding until your sister could come," I whispered the weak excuse. My heart pounded as I slowly realized the narrow corner I was being backed into, as I began to wonder, even though I didn't wish to: How soon?

"She does not matter," Donyon hissed. "She is a traitor for leaving Adelar in the first place. She sent word recently saying she plans not to return."

"I don't blame her," I muttered.

"What is that, Daughter?" my father said sternly.

"This place is like a prison." The words just spilled from me, and I trembled, quickly losing control. "If I could escape, I wouldn't come back either!"

"Gillian! That's enough—"

"I don't even have the freedom to choose who I marry!"

"So that's what this is about," Donyon snapped. "You want to break off the engagement."

"I never wanted it in the first place!"

Donyon's eyes blazed with warning. "Then why did you say that you did?"

"Because everyone else wanted it. And because I was so miserable that there seemed no way out but to just go along with it, no other choice."

"And what has changed now? Now it comes to actually having the wedding, now you find your courage to speak up?"

His words and gaze seethed at me. I glanced away, biting my lip and forcing back tears. I wanted to run. I wanted to cry. I needed some release, some way to bolt from the chains weighing more and more heavily upon me...

"If that's how you feel, then perhaps we should talk about it."

I glanced up, surprised at the sudden softness in Donyon's voice. His gaze was still hard-set with anger, determination, but also a deep hurt. I almost allowed myself to calm down, to even consider listening to Donyon, when my father broke in harshly:

"There is nothing to talk about, Donyon! I am king, and your father is lord of House Tremaine. The plans have been made since you were babes. There is nothing to discuss—!"

"That's right, father, there is nothing to discuss!" In a last desperate attempt to make my father listen, I yanked my sleeve up to remind him of the long scar stretching on my arm. I shuddered to remember one of the many fights Donyon and I had engaged in; his temper, as often, had gotten the best of him, but that time, more than his words had caused pain. I heard a gasp from Donyon as I exposed his secret and felt guilty; for a moment, it had seemed as though we'd almost begun to understand one another. But it didn't matter. At this point, I had to look out for myself. Donyon had had his chance long ago. Now he only stared, at first looking angry. Then, his gaze went blank, his expression unreadable, and he lowered his head, paling, looking suddenly ill.

The king's eyes, however, blazed furiously. "How dare you accuse with such vicious lies! That's the scar you received while you were in the woods—"

"I lied," I said flatly. "Just like I lied about wanting this marriage. But I'm not lying now. Not anymore. If you make me marry him, I will be miserable the rest of my days."

"If you don't marry him, I will see to it personally that you are."

"No," I said. "I'm done; I won't marry him! You can't make me! For once, I'm making a decision that's right for me!"

"Gillian, wait!" Donyon grabbed my arm, hard, but I jerked away, rushing from the room.

"Gillian!" my father shouted, but I ignored them all.

I rushed to my room, locked the door, and collapsed on the bed in tears. Defeated, I just lay there, wondering what it would be like if I were dead right now, and whether anyone in the castle would really care or notice. Without a daughter to pawn off in marriage, Father would just be forced to find another way to unite the Spectrum Isles into their old alliance; what a hypocrite, I finally let myself admit, that he would shun every other race of the Spectrum Isles from entering Adelar, and yet he would seek to share their power. As for Donyon, he could certainly find another lady to bend to his every whim...

I reached into my pocket, drawing out the last of Callum's letters. I touched it, stared at it, smelled it, tried to imagine him beside me, but this time, it just wasn't enough. I wanted to rush into his arms and have him hold me. I wanted to hear his voice whisper that everything would be all right.

As I reread the letter, my interest paused on something scribbled between the lines. At a glance, it looked like a few accidental ink blotches. But upon closer inspection, I recognized the marks as tiny music notes. Of course—the song. The Eagle's Song that Callum had taught me on our first meeting. I hummed it, still remembering perfectly as my eyes glanced across the notes. The eagle. The eagle was the key. The eagle was my way to freedom—and to Callum's as well.

I jumped off the bed and stormed from my room, my mind made up. It was back to the Veil. I would summon the eagle and use his powers to set both of us free.

I hurried through the corridors, dodging guards and slipping in and out of shadows here and there. There was no more need to be overly cautious. This was the last trip I would ever make to the Veil, and there would be no return journey.

I turned into the hallway where the door rested—

And froze, almost tripping over my own feet. Donyon stood before the door, blocking my path. His arms were crossed, eyes set with their hard, unsearchable edge. I had to get past him. I had to get to the eagle, for both mine and Callum's sakes.

For a long time, we stood staring at each other. My heart pounded, but I couldn't turn away, couldn't look weak. Gradually, the emptiness of Donyon's gaze filled and formed into a burning malice. I had never seen such intense hatred and I shook in fear, wondering what thoughts could create such a reaction toward me. Then, the fear blinding my thoughts subsided long enough for me to see something else beside the hatred in his eyes—an intense power, a deep concentration; I recalled his power to probe the human mind. A power I had once guarded against, but my powers had already begun to weaken with my decision to love Callum. My heart raced as I wondered just how much he had just seen.

"Oh, I've seen quite enough. Good evening, Gilly," he sneered the created nickname that I so detested.

"Good evening," I said, trying to sound calm, though my throat felt abruptly dry, and I could not release my body from its tense position.

"It grows late. Shall I escort you back to your room?"

"If you wish. I was just going back actually."

"Then why were you walking in the opposite direction?"

I remained frozen, unable to answer.

In a lightning-swift movement, he stepped forward, grabbed my arm, and wrenched my sleeve up, tearing it. I tried to break away, but his strong hand held firm, squeezing my arm. I gasped in pain, but his muscles only tightened.

"*Let go of me,*" I said in a small voice, my courage fleeing as squirmed in a vain attempt to break away.

"*Where's your mark, Gillian?*" he seethed.

"*That's none of your business—*"

"*It is every bit my business!*" he shouted, slapping me hard across the face. The blow stung. I placed my hand to my cheek to rub it and relieve the pain, but he quickly snatched that other arm, holding it just as painfully tight as the first and pushing me hard against the wall. I was forced to look up into his eyes blazing with rage.

"*Who is he, Gilly?*"

"*I don't know what you're talking about—*"

He shook me, silencing me as my head knocked against the wall. "*Your eyes—they've been changing from grey to blue for the past few weeks, and your hair darkens! Now, your mark has vanished. I know you're no longer a true Adelaran. Who did this to you? I swear, I'll kill him—*"

"*I did it to myself!*" I cried in a frightened yet still firm voice.

For a moment, he was stunned into silence.

Then, he growled, "*What do you mean?*"

"*Do not the stories of old state that if an Adelaran gives their heart and body fully to another, they become like that other, free of the Adelaran race to cling to that of their lover's?*" I spoke quietly. I was terrified, but my mind now raced for the strength and courage I so desperately needed to even be able to speak to him. I'd been so cautious in guarding my heart, despite my growing feelings for Callum —though apparently, I'd not been cautious enough when it came to the changes taking over me. Now, as my changed body attested to the truth, I allowed myself to accept and embrace it. I did love someone; I

31

had found someone. Knowing this gave me just enough courage to oppose Donyon.

"You've given yourself completely to him." Donyon's words were not a question. Rather, they were a statement made from a man on edge, threatening to explode again any moment.

I didn't tell him we had not yet been physically intimate, because it doesn't matter. I had already decided that we would be. Besides, I would not give Donyon the satisfaction of knowing that the change come over me might yet be undone.

I braced myself to be slapped again or worse.

"Your father..." Donyon breathed deeply as if trying to control himself, although his fingers only dug deeper into my arms. "We're going to see your father. We must tell him what you've done. We'll tell him you were forced, that you were out of your mind. Surely, there must be a way to reverse this..."

I stared at Donyon. I had never used my powers directly on him before, but now I was desperate; there was no more time to doubt, only act. I sang a song in my head, trying to force him to step aside—

"I don't believe it," he sneered, shaking me. "Your mind tricks won't work on me, little snake. I too have never used my powers on you, but believe me, I can do more than see truth. I can certainly use my powers to stop enemies dead in their tracks, just like your feeble little attack just now. And I can also force the truth to come out. You had best be honest with your father, because I don't want to have to do that."

He began dragging me down the hallway, but I pulled against him. "Please, there is no way to change this! Please, Donyon, telling Father will only make it worse—"

"I'll tell him you were under an enchantment, lured into the Veil against your will by some ill magic—"

"You know of the Veil?" I gasped, so surprised that I stopped resisting him.

"Of course I do. Do you think I could just sit around not knowing where you went when you weren't in your bed all those nights?"

I stared at him, dumbfounded. Despite the vicious bite in his voice, for the first time, I saw something in his eyes I'd never before seen.

Amidst the rage, anger, and frustration, there was hurt. The same hurt I'd almost allowed him to communicate to me when we were speaking with Father. And, most wondrous of all, there was love. Donyon's heart held some real feelings for me. For the first time, I felt a twinge of pity, of compassion for him. I felt angry no longer. I felt sorry for this man who thought he owned so much and yet possessed so little.

But I also felt a sickness growing in the pit of my stomach. My heart raced madly. What would Father do? He'd never understand; he'd be too furious to even try. Would he seek to take Callum's life? I knew the answer to that. But would he stop there? Did he dare declare war upon Rosa, even the entire Spectrum Isles? Despite his claims for a desire to unite the isles, I did not think such an act from him impossible, nor improbable. Why take his power by peaceful, crafty means, if he was now given reason to declare war—?

Suddenly, we were before my father's chambers, and Donyon was banging furiously on the door. It was all happening in a too-fast, surreal cacophony. My head swam with fear and dread and a nagging pain.

"Your majesty, it's me—Donyon. I have something very important I need to discuss with you!"

A great deal of shuffling of papers, stomping, and banging echoed from within. Then the king threw the door wide open. For a moment, surprise flashed upon his face, but it was soon replaced by confusion, annoyance, and then anger.

"Donyon, why are you troubling me at this late hour? And what's wrong with my daughter—she looks as though she's seen a ghost!

"Oh, she's been seeing someone all right. A filthy Rosa dog by the looks of her changing eyes—and there's this." He jerked me forward roughly, revealing the bare arm where the Adelaran mark was once imprinted.

The king could only stare again, with mounting horror and shame, and I was forced to look away from his hard stare.

"What have you done, Gillian?"

I cringed at the sudden hatred smoldering in his voice. A few tears crept into my eyes, but I fought them back.

"It wasn't her, sire," Donyon said, "She was bewitched."

"By whom?"

"I don't know, sire; she won't say."

"By whom, daughter!" my father spat. "Who did this to you?"

I almost spoke but then, as the tears threatened to rush forth, bit my lip to silence myself.

"Never mind," my father growled. "We'll destroy all the Rosa Isle if we have to, to find out who is responsible for this hideous crime. Won't we, Donyon?"

"That's right, your majesty, we will—"

34

"*No!*" *I shrieked at last, unable to take it any longer—Donyon's willingness to obey my father's mad wishes just because he was mad enough himself and had feelings enough for me to do so. I must at least try to do what I could to save Callum. And all I could do was tell the truth:*

"*No one forced themselves on me, Father. I have given myself to him.*"

The king stared as though I was some horribly diseased thing. With a snarl, he said, "Then your betrayal goes far deeper than I could have imagined. Better that you had whored yourself away to a dozen Adelaran peasants than given in to whatever witchcraft could sway you to betray your loyalties to your king, your people, and your fiancé."

I shuddered as the tears finally came. I glanced up at Donyon, begging him silently. But his stare was unreadable as stone, and he would meet neither mine nor my father's gaze.

The king turned then to Donyon and said, "How did this happen?"

"*The Veil, your majesty.*"

I felt my father's lethal gaze burning at me then as he declared, "Then let it be torn to shreds, burned, and its ashes spread upon the most desolate mountain-top."

"*Sire,*" *Donyon said, nodding, ready to obey the heart-chilling order.*

"*No!*" *I cried, trying with one, last effort to wrench away and finding, to my surprise, that I could.*

I tore down the hallway. My father shouted a command with the same coldness as though he commanded the capture of an escaped prisoner. In the next moment, Donyon's footsteps pursued.

Tears flooded my eyes, and I stumbled as they blurred my vision. Never had I run so hard in all my life. I knew Donyon's strength, that he could surpass me at any moment, yet I dare not look back.

As I rounded the corner, the door called to me, the door of the Forbidden Room. Finally, I dared to glance over my shoulder and saw no one.

I raced through the empty quiet of the room and slipped beneath the Veil, hurrying through the darkness to the moon blossom glen. The blossoms shone with milky glow in the dark night. Trembling, I lifted my head to the wind and sang out the notes of the Eagle's Song.

It echoed powerfully on the wind, echoed over and over as though I stood in a vast cavern. Nothing seemed to happen after that, and I could hear my father and Donyon fast approaching—

My father burst through the two trees, eyes wild, sword brandished as he prepared to wield vengeance on whoever had stolen his daughter's heart. The tip of his blade was already blood-stained.

The next instant, the eagle swooped down like lightning, spreading his wings wide like a shield and letting fly a victorious screech. The rush of his wings knocked Father off his feet, stunning him. I hugged one of the trees to prevent losing my own footing until the eagle had landed, so softly I did not realize at first. He stretched high, proud, and majestic, his ruby and sapphire eyes blazing with power and a perfect control of that power. I rushed over and scrambled onto his back. I leaned close to his head and breathed, "Take me to Callum."

In a movement just as swift, silent, and graceful as his landing, we sprang from the ground and soared high over the trees. I looked back one last time to see Donyon staring up at me. A red mark stained his cheek, and I prayed that he would be spared from my father's wrath.

The eagle and I surged through the midnight sky, and I looked down at the dense forest rushing by in a blur of black and green. Next, I looked behind and saw the tips of castle towers and turrets rapidly fading; beyond the castle, high cliffs stretched up. The castle was not my own, and I wondered once more where the Veil had taken me.

Then the eagle angled down sharply, and a thrill gripped me as the wind rushed past at an amazing speed. It flowed like cool, refreshing waves over my tense, weary body. It exhilarated me to move at such a great speed and height, so much so that I could not be scared. The eagle's purpose was to protect, and he would not let me fall.

We left the forest behind and zoomed over the ocean. A few minutes later, we approached a large wall of water; I knew this was one of the four barriers meant to surround and protect the Isle of Rosa, deterring outsiders. My heart leapt, and I gripped the eagle's feathers tightly. We were very close now to Callum.

The eagle burst forward at an even faster speed and began plummeting straight toward the ocean, wings spread wide, embracing the fresh, salty air. I realized just in time that he wasn't going to stop. I took a breath and put my head down. I hugged myself close to the eagle's body and clutched the feathers even tighter, bracing myself.

The cold impact of the water shocked me, and I almost took in a sharp breath but stopped myself. The force of the currents rushing against us would have knocked me off the eagle's back had I not held on so tightly. I wasn't sure then if we moved so fast that I could not breathe or if, by the eagle's power, I was able to breathe underwater. But I remained unafraid, gradually opening my eyes to see the water zipping past, glittering like sapphires. Where did the light illuminating the tiny ripples so brightly come from? Then I looked ahead: the eagle's sapphire eye radiated with a magnificent blue glow, blazing like a blue flame.

I focused my gaze forward, clinging ever more tightly to the eagle. Suddenly, I could make out a bright orange-red through the blue; we neared a new challenge. The next moment, we had catapulted from the water into a vast cave, flying at top speed toward a wall of fire. I glanced behind and saw that, by some magic, the water did not penetrate the cave, as though an invisible barrier shielded the cave's entrance.

I focused then on the wall of fire. We headed straight for the blazing barrier, but just before reaching it, the eagle's ruby eye shimmered, and bright rays of red light emanated from its glistening facets, just as the sapphire eye had done. We flew through the fire unscathed. It was amazing to be surrounded by fire, to be so close to something so dangerous yet know I had nothing to fear. Slowly, I sat up on the eagle's back, gazing about in full wonder.

The eagle surged straight up. The starry sky spread above, tumbling nearer and nearer. Then we emerged from the cavern, and the water wall barrier I'd seen from the sky rose before us. No wonder no one could get into Rosa. To even get to this visible barrier we now approached, one had to know about the two that were hidden under the ocean. Even then, it would take the most powerful magic to match the eagle's and brave the elements of fire and water.

We plunged through the high wall of water, and I braced myself for the impact. But this time, I felt none. The oddest thing was to stretch out my hand and feel the water, but beyond that, to remain perfectly dry.

After the wall of water, the last barrier loomed, a wall just as high, blue flames smoldering with majestic challenge. The blue fire was even hotter, even more intense, than that we'd just passed through. Though we again passed unharmed, I could feel some of the heat radiating from its inferno.

Finally, we were through. The moment we emerged from the flames, I saw the castle of Rosa situated on a high hill, overlooking the entire city.

The eagle sped straight toward the castle and swooped around to one of the towers. A dim orange glow shone from beyond the bars covering a single small window. The eagle hovered just long enough for me to spot a person's silhouette by the window and to hear Callum gasp, "Gillian?"

Then, the eagle clutched the iron bars in its talons, and I shouted, "Callum, get back!" The eagle pulled on the bars, and I released a small yelp as his feathers stretched up into streamers of red and blue flames. I could feel the eagle's heat blazing vehemently all around me, but I again felt no pain. The fire crept from the bird's feathers and down into its feet. They glowed bright red like iron about to be molded. Then the iron bars themselves gleamed the same brilliant hue until, with a final tug and a victorious shriek, the eagle bent the bars and pulled them from the window, flinging them aside.

Moments later, Callum was hurrying up to the window. He bent down and positioned himself in the small window frame. I reached out my hand to him, but as he took my hand and started to crawl onto the eagle's back, he cried out. I screamed as the eagle swept backwards, away from the window; Callum had tumbled from the window and held to the ledge by one hand. I urged the eagle forward, *but when the bird jerked backward, almost knocking me off, I looked up and saw the arrow lodged fast in its wing. I glanced up at the two soldiers leaning out the window, struggling to pull Callum back in while he fought them. Suddenly, their grasp slipped, and he fell.*

My scream was silenced as the eagle catapulted downward, catching Callum in its powerful claws. We were soaring across the ocean even before we could hear the faint gonging of a bell sounding the alarm of his escape.

After a long while, another island rose up before us, and the eagle swooped low, stumbling onto its sandy shores. I tumbled off his back and then rushed to Callum who'd landed several feet away.

Callum was sitting up, brushing sand from his clothes. For a moment, I stood over him, watching, and he looked up, incredulous. Then, he stood to his feet, touched my cheek, and said, "That was amazing. I truly know now how Amiel has led you to me for a purpose—"

The eagle released a shrill cry, and Callum and I turned in the bird's direction. The eagle stretched his right wing wide, displaying two small marks where the arrows had stuck; streams of blood trickled down. I wondered what had become of the arrows; perhaps the eagle's body had still been hot enough to burn them to ash. At any rate, while the arrows hadn't impeded the creature's flight too much, I knew that the leftover wounds must sting terribly.

Callum and I raced over, and I said, "Stay here with him. I will go into the woods, find some asplas plant to heal the wounds."

It didn't take me long to find the plant. Once I had grabbed a large handful, I hurried back to the beach. Callum helped me rub the plant into the eagle's wounds. At first, he screeched, wincing in pain. But the more deeply we rubbed the plant and its cooling medicines inside the bird's wounds, the more he calmed. Eventually, he sat very still and then lay on the sand, watching us with a grateful submission and peace.

Callum collapsed on the sand then, and I fell beside him.

"So," I said, "what now?"

"Now?" Callum took a deep breath, glanced back at the wood. "Well, we can't stay here. This is Loz, and I have made too many friends here, and the Rosa guard knows it. I would not seek to endanger anyone here, nor would it be wise, for our own safety, to linger here.

"However, I do have a friend who lives in Loz, who could grant us a safe place, I believe, in Abalino."

"Abalino," I breathed, filled with wonder despite my tiredness. "The city in the sky?"

Callum nodded. "No one will look for us there, I think. From there, we can more safely and strategically pick up from where I left off in planning the rebellion. There are still plenty of allies from all over the surrounding islands, those who believe in our cause—"

"The rebellion?" I echoed, still stuck on his mention of it. I couldn't quite tell whether I felt skeptical about his mentioning it, or just incredulous, or some mixture of the two. Daring to speak of it seemed insane after what we'd just been through. Then again, I admired his perseverance, and freedom was my entire reason for rescuing us in the first place. The rebellion was simply an extension of our desire to obtain freedom; besides, by the look on Callum's face, continuing his work was as natural for him as breathing. I couldn't even suggest trying to stifle that part of him—nor would he likely let me.

Callum nodded again. "The rebellion has seen some challenges and some losses, but we hold firm to what we believe in. Our trials will pave the way for the freedom of others. I will grant you protection no matter what you choose but, especially after witnessing your bravery tonight, I would wish that you join with us. I believe you could be a great asset to our cause."

"I'm not so sure if I was brave or just reckless," I admitted. "But, I will gladly join your cause. Your cause and mine—they are the same. They always were."

★ *Beyond the Veil* is a part of *The Gailean Quartet*, which Schulze is rewriting alongside her brilliant editor, Kira Lerner. Schulze expects to start releasing new editions of the series in 2016.

Dear Readers,

I would love to hear from you—no, I really, really would!

One of my favorite things about being an author is getting the opportunity to meet, speak with, and get to know my readers on a more personal level. What truly excites me about being an author today is that there are a variety of ways authors and readers can easily connect with one another.

If you enjoyed the story you just read—or even if you didn't—feel free to leave an honest review at any of these websites: Goodreads, Barnes and Noble, and/or Amazon. Hopping online to see what my readers have to say about my books really motivates me as an author. Whether you absolutely loved the story, have constructive criticism to give, or simply want to share your thoughts with friends and family about the new author you've just discovered, any feedback is appreciated and helps me out! I am also donating twenty-five percent of all royalties to ALFA, a local charity that helps fund programs for adults with disabilities, so spreading the word about my books ultimately helps them as well.

If you have any questions for me or just want to say "hello," you can find me on Facebook or Goodreads. Also, at my website: http://christineschulze.com

Or, if you're old fashioned like me and enjoy writing letters, you can reach me at the following:

Email: ChristineESchulze@gmail.com

Snail Mail: Christine E. Schulze
18 Archview Drive
Belleville, IL 62221

Thanks so much for your support! I look forward to hearing from you and hope we can share in many more adventures together.

~ Christine E. Schulze

The Amielian Legacy

The Amielian Legacy is a vast fantasy comprised of both stand-alone books and series for ages ranging from children to young adult. *The Amielian Legacy* creates a fantastical history for North America in much the same way that Tolkien's Middle Earth created a mythology for Europe. While it's not necessary to read any particular book or series to read the others, they do ultimately weave together to create a single overarching mythology.

Stand-Alone Books
Bloodmaiden (Second Edition)
Lily in the Snow (Second Edition)
Larimar: Gem of the Sea
Dream Catcher, Heart Listener
Beyond the Veil
Follow Me
Tears of a Vampire Prince
The Chronicles of the Mira
The Crystal Rings
Song Quest
Black Lace/Dark Embrace
The Adventures of William the Brownie
In the Land of Giants
The Amazing K
The Pirates of Meleeon
The Last Star (No release date yet)
Carousel in the Clouds (No release date yet)

Series
The Stregoni Sequence
Golden Healer, Dark Enchantress
Memory Charmer
Wish Granter

A Shadow Beyond Time (with co-author Kira Lerner)
The Undying Portal (No release date yet)
The Awakening Army (No release date yet)
The Mourning Birds (No release date yet)
The Darkling Shadow (No release date yet)
The Bleeding Veil (No release date yet)

The Gailean Quartet (Second Editions; first release 2016)

The Legends of Surprisers
The Legends of Surprisers, Book I (No release date yet)
The Legends of Surprisers, Book II (No release date yet)
The Legends of Surprisers, Book III: The Vision (No release date yet)

D.N.A. Sequence (No release date yet)